Not a Penny More, Not a Penny Less

JEFFREY ARCHER

Level 3

Retold by Annette Barnes
Series Editor: Derek Strange

PENGUIN BOOKS

PENGUIN BOOKS

Published by the Penguin Group
Penguin Books Ltd, 27 Wrights Lane, London W8 5TZ, England
Penguin Books USA Inc., 375 Hudson Street, New York, New York 10014, USA
Penguin Books Australia Ltd, Ringwood, Victoria, Australia
Penguin Books Canada Ltd, 10 Alcorn Avenue, Toronto, Ontario, Canada M4V 3B2
Penguin Books (NZ) Ltd, 182–190 Wairau Road, Auckland 10, New Zealand

Penguin Books Ltd, Registered Offices: Harmondsworth, Middlesex, England

First published by Jonathan Cape Ltd 1976
This adaptation published by Penguin Books 1996
1 3 5 7 9 10 8 6 4 2

Illustrations by David Cuzik (Pennant Illustration Agency)

Printed in England by Clays Ltd, St Ives plc
Set in 11/14 pt Lasercomp Bembo by
Datix International Limited, Bungay, Suffolk

To the teacher:

In addition to all the language forms of Levels One and Two, which are used again at this level of the series, the main verb forms and tenses used at Level Three are:

- past continuous verbs, present perfect simple verbs, conditional clauses (using the 'first' or 'open future' conditional), question tags and further common phrasal verbs
- modal verbs: *have (got) to* and *don't have to* (to express obligation), *need to* and *needn't* (to express necessity), *could* and *was able to* (to describe past ability), *could* and *would* (in offers and polite requests for help, and *shall* (for future plans, offers and suggestions).

Also used are:

- relative pronouns: *who*, *that* and *which* (in defining clauses)
- conjunctions: *if* and *since* (for time or reason), *so that* (for purpose or result) and *while*
- indirect speech (questions)
- participle clauses.

Specific attention is paid to vocabulary development in the Vocabulary Work exercises at the end of the book. These exercises are aimed at training students to enlarge their vocabulary systematically through intelligent reading and effective use of a dictionary.

To the student:

Dictionary Words:

- When you read this book, you will find that some words are darker black than the others on the page. Look them up in your dictionary, if you do not already know them, or try to guess the meaning of the words first, without a **dictionary**.

'We'll both be very rich by this time next year.'

CHAPTER ONE

It was David Kesler's first time in England and everything seemed very small after New York. He was taking the train from London to Oxford to visit an old friend from Harvard University. David was looking forward to seeing Stephen Bradley again but he was more excited about his new job with Prospecta Oil. In his hand was a report about oil in the North Sea and David read it again while the train travelled towards Oxford.

'There's no mistake,' he thought. 'Anyone who puts money into Prospecta Oil is going to be very rich.'

♦

'. . . but my father died last winter,' said Stephen. He pushed his glasses higher on his nose. 'Perhaps you can help me, David. He left me a lot of money and it's still just sitting in the bank. I don't know much about business or the best way to use the money.'

David was happy to be able to help an old friend and he told Stephen about the report for Prospecta Oil.

'Why don't you use your money there? I'm going to buy some of these **shares**. The price of the shares will go up a lot when everyone knows about this report and when the time is right we can sell them. We'll both be very rich by this time next year.'

Stephen looked at the report David had with him. Yes, it seemed like a very good idea, he thought.

When Stephen Bradley bought his shares, they cost £3.10 each and he bought 40,000.

♦

Back in London, David Kesler told a few other people about Prospecta Oil and slowly the price of the shares went up. By the end of the week they cost £3.73 each. David's boss in Boston USA was pleased. Thanks to David, Prospecta Oil shares were selling fast. He decided to give David another $5,000 because he was doing a good job. David wanted to buy a picture with the money and while he was looking he met some other people who were interested in Prospecta Oil. The price of the shares went up again, to £3.90 each. One week later they cost £4.80.

♦

The following Monday David arrived at work and found the office locked and empty. Nobody from Prospecta Oil was there. He phoned his bank and asked about the price of Prospecta Oil shares.

'They've gone down to £3.80 but I don't know why. I'll ask some questions and call you back.'

'Sell my shares now,' said David. He didn't understand what was happening and felt sick when he remembered his conversations with Stephen and other people.

On Wednesday morning the share price was down to £1 and at the end of the day to 25p.

David was very worried and he didn't know what to do next. He went to the bank and took out all his money. When he got to his flat a neighbour spoke to him.

'The police were here looking for you.'

David was frightened now. The only thing he wanted to do was to get out of London. He put everything into his suitcases, drove to the airport and bought a one-way ticket to New York.

♦

In Oxford, Stephen bought the morning newspaper and couldn't understand what he read about Prospecta Oil. He tried to telephone David but there was no answer. In the evening two policeman came to see him.

'David Kesler has left the country, but we don't think he had any idea what was happening. The man who started Prospecta Oil is Harvey Metcalfe. He lives in the USA. But there is no oil and no **company** now.'

'But I saw the report on North Sea oil; it said the oil was there,' said Stephen.

'Yes, it was very clever. But it didn't say that there really *was* oil where Prospecta were looking, just that there *probably* was. You bought Harvey Metcalfe's shares and so did other people. Because you were all buying, the price went up and up. He sold all his shares and got your money, then closed the offices and walked away. And his name won't be on any papers, you can be sure of that. Prospecta Oil is only a company on paper now. There's nothing more.'

Stephen was angry with himself. It was a stupid thing to do and now all his father's money was gone.

'Can you tell me anything about this Harvey Metcalfe?' he asked.

'He lives in Boston, he's very rich, very clever and not very honest. He's given a lot of money to Harvard University over the years, but he's kept much more for himself. David Kesler probably never met him or spoke to him.'

Stephen had another question.

'Am I the only person who lost a lot of money?'

'No, sir. There were three other men who bought about the same number of shares as you did. Kesler met them all in London.'

'Can you tell me their names?'

'There was a Harley Street doctor, Dr Robin Oakley; a

Frenchman, Jean-Pierre Lamanns of the Lamanns **Gallery** in Bond Street and **Lord** James Brigsley. He borrowed money to buy the shares and the bank will take his family farm if he can't pay them back. It's very bad luck. Together, you lost about $1 million.'

♦

In the next few days Stephen found a lot of information about Harvey Metcalfe. Then he found the addresses of the other three men and sent them each a letter that asked them to come to Oxford for dinner. At the bottom of the letters he wrote 'David Kesler won't be able to come.'

♦

The first to arrive was Jean-Pierre Lamanns and then Robin Oakley and then James Brigsley. It was a mystery to them all why Stephen wanted to meet them. But they soon understood.

'We've all lost a lot of money in Prospecta Oil. I think if we work together, we can get it all back,' Stephen told them after a very good dinner in his rooms.

They were all surprised and thought Stephen was stupid to think about trying to do it.

'It's impossible,' said Jean-Pierre.

'Harvey Metcalfe is very clever; he's an **expert** at this. How can we win against him?' asked Robin.

Stephen gave them each an envelope of papers with all his information about Harvey Metcalfe.

'We can win because we're all experts too, at other things that he doesn't understand. I know a lot about this man now and I think we can get our money back from him. And he'll never know what we've done,' he said.

He read from the first paper.

'Every year, Harvey comes to Europe for a holiday. In

Stephen gave them each an envelope of papers with all his information about Harvey Metcalfe.

England he goes to see the tennis at Wimbledon, he watches the horse **races** at Ascot and he visits the London galleries because he buys pictures. He also spends some time in Monte Carlo. In all these places we are more at home than he is.'

Stephen picked up the other papers.

'These papers tell you everything about Harvey Metcalfe. Please study them carefully and each think of a plan for how to get our money back. There will be four different plans and we'll all help with each plan. If we work together, we can get all the money back – not a penny more, not a penny less. We'll meet here again in fourteen days.'

Robin and Jean-Pierre still weren't sure about Stephen's idea but James said, 'I agree. Together maybe we can do this.'

♦

On the way home, both Robin and Jean-Pierre started to think of ideas but James sat in the train to London and couldn't think of anything. Sitting opposite him was a beautiful girl and he tried to think how to start a conversation with her. Then he noticed that the woman next to her was reading a magazine and he was surprised to see a photo of the same girl on the front. When the other woman got off the train he asked her about the picture.

'Sometimes it's very boring, always smiling for photographs,' she said, 'but I go to some interesting places.'

She told him her name, Anne Summerton. She lived in London but her parents were American. When the train arrived in London, James drove her home and asked her for her telephone number.

He was not thinking about Harvey Metcalfe now.

She told him her name, Anne Summerton. She lived in London but her parents were American.

'You must have a plan ready when we meet again in three weeks, James.'

CHAPTER TWO

It was two weeks later and all four men were again sitting in Stephen's room at Oxford University. Stephen had some more information about Harvey. Now they knew when he would arrive in England, which hotel he was staying at and when he would go to Monte Carlo. They also knew when he was returning to America.

Next they had to decide which plan to do, where and when. Robin wanted Monte Carlo for his plan, Jean-Pierre wanted Wimbledon and Stephen wanted Ascot and a few days before Harvey went home to America. James didn't have a plan yet. He was trying to think of one, but he still had no ideas. Stephen was angry with him.

'You must have a plan ready when we meet again in three weeks, James. Now, we'll hear the others. Robin, you first . . .'

♦

The next few weeks were very busy. They all had to go to hospital with Robin to learn how doctors work, James had to practise driving fast through the city and Jean-Pierre had to learn all about playing cards in a **casino**. Stephen went back to Oxford for a week to find more information about the Secretary of the University's office. Everyone had to practise using a two-way radio and trying to make themselves look different. Stephen started to grow a moustache. Their plans were nearly ready – but James still didn't have a plan. He was too busy seeing Anne. One evening he told her about what they were doing but he didn't tell the others that Anne knew. She promised to help him think of a plan.

♦

Harvey arrived in London. On the first day of Wimbledon, he went to watch the tennis. The game that he watched wasn't very interesting so after half an hour he got up and walked out. Robin was sitting opposite him and he followed Harvey when he left. Harvey's car took him into London, to Bond Street. Robin drove behind him, telling the others on his radio where they were. Jean-Pierre had a special picture to put into the window of his gallery when he knew Harvey was near. The picture looked just like a Van Gogh but it wasn't a real one.

At Bond Street, Harvey left his car and started visiting galleries, looking for a picture to buy. He felt happy.

'Maybe today's my lucky day,' he thought. 'First my wife phoned, then my daughter. I feel sure this is the day that I'm going to find a wonderful picture.'

Behind him, Robin spoke into his radio.

'He's getting near your gallery, put the Van Gogh in now, Jean-Pierre . . . he's stopped to look at something in another window . . . getting very near now . . .'

Harvey walked up to the window of the Lamanns Gallery and stopped. He was very surprised to see the Van Gogh in the centre of the window. It was beautiful; he wanted it immediately.

He walked inside and Jean-Pierre, Stephen and James were talking about the picture.

'. . . disappeared in Berlin in 1937,' said Jean-Pierre.

When Stephen spoke Harvey thought he was foreign. He had a moustache now and the colour of his hair was darker too so he looked quite different to usual. His voice sounded German. He spoke to Jean-Pierre, '£170,000 seems expensive, but it's beautiful. I'll get the money from my bank and return at 4 p.m.'

'You're a lucky man, Herr Drosser,' said James. 'If you

Harvey walked up to the window of the Lamanns Gallery and stopped.

decide to sell it one day, please telephone me.' James gave Stephen a card with his address on.

'Where shall we send the picture?' asked Jean-Pierre. 'Where are you staying in London?'

'The Dorchester Hotel, room 120,' said Stephen, then he said goodbye and left the gallery.

Harvey surprised everyone then. Instead of trying to buy the picture for more money, he walked out behind Stephen. At first they didn't know what to do next.

They had to think quickly. Robin told Stephen on his radio about Harvey. James quickly found a taxi and got to the Dorchester before Stephen. He paid for room 120 and gave Stephen the key when he walked in. Stephen went up to room 120 and very soon, Harvey came into the hotel. At the desk he asked for Herr Drosser.

'Room 120, I think,' the man said. Then Harvey spoke to Stephen on the telephone and asked to meet him.

Stephen waited in room 120 and a few minutes later Harvey knocked at the door.

'Herr Drosser,' said Harvey, 'I know that you have just bought a Van Gogh and I'm very interested in buying it from you. Will you sell it to me for more than you paid?'

'I don't think so. I want it for my gallery in Munich,' said Stephen.

'You paid £170,000. That's about $405,000. I'll pay you $15,000 more,' said Harvey.

Stephen thought for a minute. He knew he could make Harvey pay more.

'$20,000 more, and I'll agree,' he said.

Harvey didn't speak. Stephen waited.

'OK, $20,000 more,' said Harvey.

Stephen phoned Jean-Pierre at the gallery.

'I have a Mr Metcalfe here with me. He will come into the

Stephen thought for a minute. He knew he could make Harvey pay more. '$20,000 more, and I'll agree,' he said.

gallery in the next few minutes and pay you for the Van Gogh. Please give him the picture.'

At the other end of the telephone Jean-Pierre guessed what was happening and laughed quietly.

In room 120 Harvey Metcalfe gave Stephen $20,000.

'Thank you, I'm a very happy man now,' he said.

'And I am not too unhappy,' said Stephen. They shook hands and Harvey left the hotel.

Stephen called Robin and James on their radios and by the time Jean-Pierre arrived at the hotel the three of them were already in the bar with a bottle of **champagne**.

One down and three to go.

♦

Their next meeting was at James's London flat where they had to talk about Robin's plan for Monte Carlo. Robin gave them some more things to do.

'Jean-Pierre, you must shave off your moustache, start growing a beard and cut your hair short. It's very important that Harvey doesn't realize who you are. How's the driving going James?'

'I think I'll be able to do the journey in about eleven minutes, but I'll have to practise some more when we get to Monte Carlo.'

'Good. Now, Stephen has been a very good student at the hospital. Are you happy about helping me to **operate** on Harvey?' asked Robin.

Stephen said he was.

'And I'm pleased that he'll be asleep most of the time that I'm with him. I don't want him to remember Herr Drosser,' he said. They all laughed.

Robin looked at his papers again.

'We're flying to Nice on Monday, the same day that

Harvey is arriving in Monte Carlo on his boat. We won't sit together on the plane, or take the same taxi from the airport. We've got four rooms in the same hotel, near the casino. Everything is ready for us at the hospital when we want it and I'll telephone them at the right time to say we're bringing Harvey in,' he told them.

Stephen looked at James, who still had no plan.

'The most important thing for you to do, James, is to think of your idea. You must have a plan soon.'

Then they all went home.

James said goodbye to everyone and went back into his kitchen where Anne was waiting.

'Did you listen?' he asked her.

'Yes,' she said, 'and they all sounded very nice. They're right, you must think of a plan quickly. We've got more than a week before Mr Metcalfe goes to Monte Carlo. Perhaps I can help you to think of something.'

♦

The next week they flew to Nice. James was worried because he still didn't have a plan, but he was still thinking.

After they arrived at the hotel in Monte Carlo they met in Robin's room. Jean-Pierre then went to the casino to watch Harvey and James walked from the casino to the hospital. Then he went to find Harvey's boat. Robin and Stephen went to the hospital and made sure that there was an ambulance ready for them. Robin told the doctor at the hospital who he was.

'I'm Doctor Wiley Barker of the University of California,' he said, in an American voice.

Everything was now ready for Robin's plan.

CHAPTER THREE

On their first night in Monte Carlo Harvey didn't go to the casino until very late and Jean-Pierre couldn't get a place next to him. On the second night Harvey arrived at the casino with a friend. But on the next night they had better luck.

Jean-Pierre was already playing cards at the casino when Harvey arrived and sat next to him, in the place that he always used. After a few minutes Harvey ordered a cup of black coffee and the waiter put it between him and Jean-Pierre. As he played, Harvey watched a young man on the other side of him who was losing a lot of money.

Jean-Pierre took his handkerchief from his pocket and at the same time he quickly put a pill into Harvey's coffee. Then he finished the game and walked away from the table to the bar. Stephen was already waiting in the bar. Jean-Pierre called James and Robin on their radios. Then they all waited.

At first, Harvey just felt a little sick, so he stayed at the table. He ordered another coffee but that didn't help and his stomach started to hurt more and more. About an hour later it was so bad that he decided he must leave. When he tried to get up from the table he fell onto the floor. People quickly came round him to see what was happening. Suddenly Stephen pushed through the people.

'Stand back, please. I'm a doctor,' he said.

Harvey was feeling terrible.

'My stomach . . . hurts . . . very badly . . .' he said.

Stephen quickly opened Harvey's shirt.

'Where does it hurt most?'

Harvey showed him and Stephen touched the place on his stomach. Harvey screamed loudly.

Jean-Pierre took his handkerchief from his pocket and at the same time he quickly put a pill into Harvey's coffee.

'You'll have to go to hospital. Let's hope there's a doctor there and he can operate immediately.'

Jean-Pierre spoke at just the right time.

'Dr Wiley Barker is staying at my hotel – the famous American doctor.'

Stephen looked at Harvey.

'He'll be very expensive, sir,' he said.

Harvey screamed again.

'It doesn't matter how much . . . get him . . . I want the best . . .' Then he **fainted**.

Stephen spoke to Jean-Pierre.

'Please call Dr Barker and ask him to go to the hospital quickly. And call for an ambulance.'

Jean-Pierre ran out of the casino and called Robin and James. Robin took a taxi straight to the hospital and James drove the ambulance very fast through Monte Carlo to the Casino. He arrived there eleven minutes later and together they took Harvey out to the ambulance and then to the hospital. In the ambulance Stephen and Jean-Pierre changed into hospital clothes. Robin was waiting when they arrived.

They all knew what to do. Stephen gave Harvey some gas and they all got ready to help Robin operate. Jean-Pierre gave Robin a knife.

He made a long cut in Harvey's stomach. Then he closed the cut again. He didn't have to do anything more to him but it must look real when Harvey saw it.

They cleaned his stomach and Stephen gave him a little more gas. Then James brought the ambulance to the front of the hospital and they carried Harvey to it. Stephen changed out of his hospital clothes and went to the telephone while James drove the others slowly to Harvey's boat. A nurse was waiting for them there.

Stephen telephoned the local newspaper and told them the

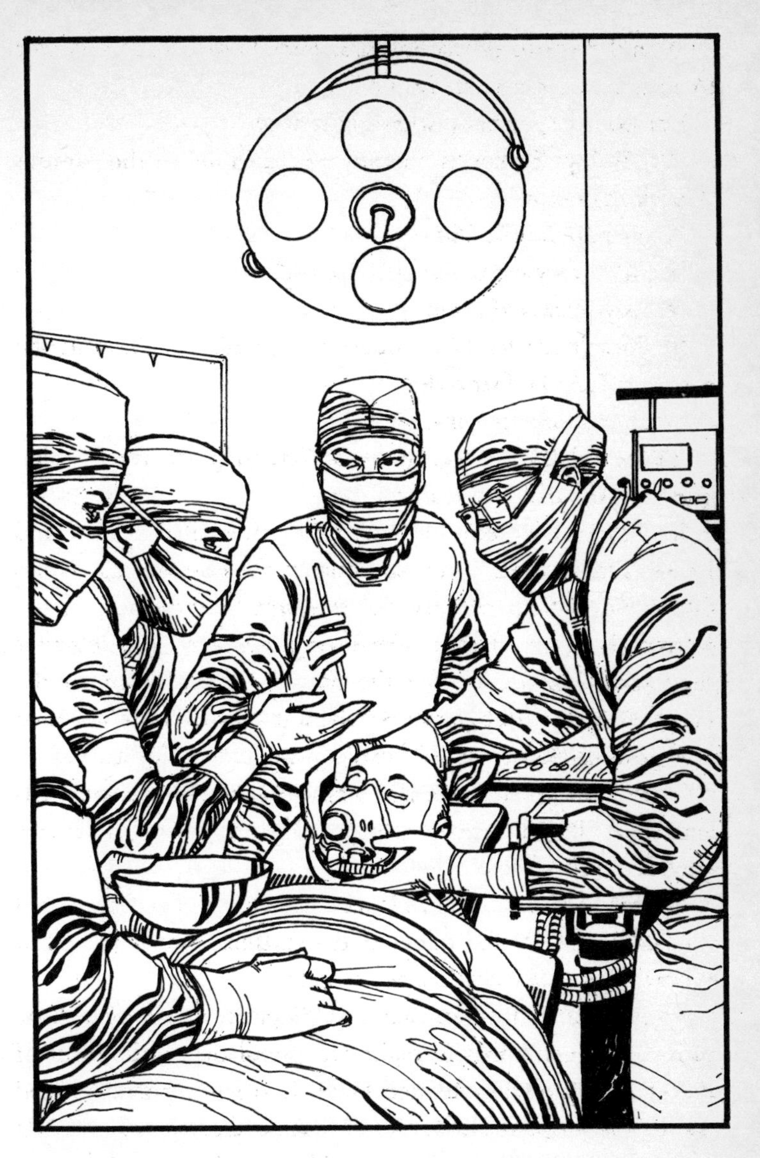

Stephen gave Harvey some gas and they all got ready to help Robin operate.

story of Harvey's visit to hospital. They were all back at the hotel by 3.30 a.m.

♦

The next morning at eleven Robin was ready to visit Harvey on his boat. He was a little worried about meeting him, but he knew he looked just right. He was wearing small round glasses and his hair was cut short.

Harvey was sitting up in bed and was very pleased to see Robin.

'I've just telephoned my wife, Dr Barker, and told her all about it. You saved me from dying. In the newspaper it says I had a **private** ambulance and you operated on me immediately. Of course, I don't remember a thing.'

Robin was very pleased to hear that.

'Tell me, Doctor, was I really in danger?'

'Oh yes, you're lucky I was able to operate so quickly,' said Robin.

'I can't thank you enough Dr Barker. If you want me to do anything for you any time, just ask. Now, this nurse that you found me – is she good? I'd prefer you to see me each day until I'm better.'

Robin didn't know what to say at first because that wasn't part of the plan.

'Of course, I'll pay. I'm happy to pay for the best doctor.'

Robin thought quickly.

'It's possible it will be as much as $80,000.'

'OK, OK. That's not a lot to stay alive.'

They shook hands and Robin left the boat and went back to the hotel. They were all waiting for him in Stephen's room when he arrived.

'I'm staying here for another week,' he told them. 'And we're getting $80,000 for it.'

'Of course, I'll pay. I'm happy to pay for the best doctor.'

Everyone was very proud of Robin.

♦

After six days Harvey was well again and Robin went to say goodbye to him.

'I'm going to Ascot next week, Doctor. Will you be able to come for the day? My horse Rosalie is running.'

'I'm very sorry, I have to return to California. But I hope she wins her race for you.'

Robin flew back to England that day with Harvey's $80,000 in his pocket.

Two down and two to go.

♦

The next Friday they all met in Robin's office. They still had to get $494,970 from Harvey.

'So we must talk about my plan,' Stephen said, 'which starts in Ascot. After Ascot we'll have time to practise the next part of the plan before we get Harvey in Oxford. And I'm very worried because James still hasn't got a plan. We must think of something soon because when Harvey goes back to America it will be much more difficult.'

They all promised to help James find a plan.

'Now,' said Stephen, 'for Ascot I shall have grey hair and Jean-Pierre, you must shave off that beard and wear glasses. Make sure Harvey doesn't see you too much. For Oxford of course we'll all need grey hair. We must look much older. Remember, Harvey has seen us all before now, so we must look quite different.'

An hour later Robin had to start work again. Jean-Pierre went back to his gallery and every night he practised his part in the Oxford plan. Stephen went back to Oxford.

James took Anne to Stratford-upon-Avon for the weekend

and they went to the theatre. That evening, when they were walking by the river, he asked her to marry him and she said yes.

He still couldn't think of a plan. But Anne was beginning to get an idea . . .

♦

Stephen, James and Jean-Pierre met at a pub near Ascot. Robin had to stay in London to send Harvey a **telegram**. James was the first to go to Ascot and when he saw Harvey's car arrive he called the others on his radio.

'He's going into his private room,' he told them. On the door it said 'Mr Harvey Metcalfe and Friends' and James knew there was lunch and champagne there for everyone. Stephen and Jean-Pierre met James outside.

A telegram arrived for Harvey, from his daughter.

'It's from Rosalie,' he said, 'it's nice of her to remember about the race. I named the horse after her, of course, and they're both beautiful.' He laughed.

Another telegram arrived, this time from London. Harvey read it to his friends.

'"Sorry I can't come to Ascot; if you see my old friend **Professor** Rodney Porter, please look after him." It's from Dr Wiley Barker, the man who saved me in Monte Carlo.'

He walked towards the door.

'I've got to try to find this Professor Porter,' he said and left the room.

Stephen's plan was starting.

'Professor Porter, how nice to see you again.' He shook hands with Stephen.

CHAPTER FOUR

When Jean-Pierre saw Harvey in the crowd outside his room he went up to Stephen and said in a very loud voice, 'Professor Porter, how nice to see you again.'

He shook hands with Stephen, they said a few words and then Jean-Pierre walked away. Harvey came straight across to Stephen and told him about the telegram.

'So I want you to come to my private room and have some champagne with me,' he said.

They watched the races together and talked about Harvey's horse, Rosalie. Harvey was very pleased and excited when Rosalie won her race. Stephen spent the rest of the day with Harvey and before they said goodbye he asked him to come to Oxford the next Wednesday. Stephen explained that it was a special day at the university because it was the end of the summer term. There was a garden party and a lot of other things happening. Harvey was very happy because he wanted to see Oxford and the university, so he said yes.

♦

During the next few days in Oxford, they practised Stephen's plan again and again. It had to be perfect because they could only try it once. Every second was important.

Stephen was awake early on Wednesday, and spent a long time in front of the mirror making himself look much older. Then he dressed and put on his red **gown**. On that day in Oxford there were a lot of people wearing gowns and Stephen had got some for the others to wear.

He met Harvey at his hotel and told him about the first thing that they would see.

'I think they're hoping maybe you'll give the university something after your win at Ascot races last week.'

'There's a special breakfast for all the important people at the university; then they walk through the city to the theatre. We can go and see that first. Then in the theatre they give special gowns to people who have helped the university . . . with money, you know. They're called Doctors of Letters.'

Harvey was very interested in this. 'I'd really like to see that,' he said.

'You can,' said Stephen. 'Because you're so interested in Harvard University and you've given them a lot of money I was able to get us tickets.'

'That's wonderful,' Harvey said. He was enjoying himself a lot. 'What happens after that?' he asked.

'They all go to a special lunch.'

'We can have lunch at my hotel.'

'No,' said Stephen, 'we're going with them. I think they're hoping maybe you'll give the university something after your win at Ascot races last week.'

'What a great idea,' said Harvey. 'Why didn't I think of that?'

They spent the morning together and enjoyed the special lunch. All the important people in the university were there and Harvey loved it. Stephen could see his plan was going very well.

There was an hour before the garden party started and Stephen said, 'Shall we look at some of the university buildings?' and he took Harvey away from all the other people to the place where he knew Robin was waiting. They walked round the corner and there was Robin. He looked quite old with grey hair and a grey moustache. He was wearing a black and red gown. Stephen stopped and spoke to Robin.

'Vice-Chancellor*, I'd like you to meet Mr Harvey Metcalfe, from Boston.

Harvey shook hands with Robin.

'I hope you're enjoying your visit to Oxford, Mr Metcalfe.'

'I am very much and I'd like to help the university, if I can.'

'That's very good news,' said Robin.

'Perhaps you can have tea with me at my hotel this afternoon,' said Harvey.

Stephen and Robin were quiet for a few seconds. This wasn't part of the plan. Robin thought quickly.

'It's difficult for me on a busy day like this, Mr Metcalfe, but if you come to my rooms at the Clarendon Building at about 4.30 perhaps we can have a private conversation then? I shall ask the Secretary of the University and the Registrar** to come too.'

Harvey agreed immediately. He was very excited about meeting the Vice-Chancellor.

When Stephen and Harvey walked past a shop in the High Street, they saw a red and blue gown in the window. Stephen could see what Harvey was thinking.

'You have to be a Doctor of Letters at the university to wear that. Would you like to try it on?'

They went into the shop and Harvey tried on the gown. He thought it looked wonderful.

'What do they cost?' he asked Stephen.

'About £100 I think.'

* Vice-Chancellor: A very important person in the university but not a professor. He or she is the head of the university offices.

** Registrar: This person is almost as important as the Vice-Chancellor. The Registrar's office looks after the university's reports and papers.

They went into the shop and Harvey tried on the gown.

'No, I mean – how much do I have to give to the university to be a Doctor of Letters?'

'I really don't know. Perhaps you can talk to the Vice-Chancellor about it this afternoon.'

While Harvey was putting his jacket on again Stephen quietly paid for the gown and asked them to send it to the Clarendon Building.

Then they went to the garden party.

♦

At 4.30 Stephen and Harvey arrived at the Clarendon Building. The real Vice-Chancellor was still at the garden party so there was nobody there to see them.

They went upstairs and met Robin and Jean-Pierre. Suddenly, the door opened behind them and a very old man of about ninety came in.

'Where's this man Metcalfe?' he shouted to Jean-Pierre. It was James, but it was very difficult to **recognize** him.

'Is this him, Registrar?' he said and pointed at Harvey. 'I have read about you, Mr Metcalfe.'

'Mr Metcalfe, this is the Secretary of the University,' said Stephen.

They talked for a few minutes then Harvey said, 'I'm very proud to be here today. This has been a wonderful year for me. I bought a Van Gogh in London, my horse won at Ascot and the best doctor in America operated on me when I was ill in Monte Carlo. My horse Rosalie won nearly $250,000 and now I want to give it to this great university.'

'We'll take it,' shouted James, 'But nobody must know. That's the way we do things in Oxford, you know.'

Harvey agreed, and Jean-Pierre went out of the room to get the gown. They put it on Harvey's shoulders and he smiled at everyone.

'Wonderful,' he said. 'Just wonderful'.

Three down and one to go.

♦

James hurried back to London to meet Anne for dinner and to meet her father for the first time. He went to his flat to change his clothes and make himself look thirty-five again instead of ninety. Then he drove to the restaurant where a private room was ready for them for dinner. Anne met him outside.

'James, come in and meet my father.'

He followed her into the room.

'How are you, my boy? I've heard so much about you from Rosalie, I can't wait to get to know you.'

They shook hands and James suddenly felt faint.

'You must call me Harvey. I can't believe my daughter's going to marry a real Lord, our Rosalie . . .'

'James knows me as Anne, Daddy.'

'I don't understand why you had to change your name for work,' said Harvey.

'No, I don't either,' said James. He could see that Harvey didn't recognize him so he was beginning to feel better.

'Most of my friends have changed their names for work. Also, in my job it's not very good that you named a horse after me, Daddy.'

During dinner Harvey told James all about his holiday in England and Monte Carlo. Then they talked about the plans for James and Anne's wedding in Boston.

After they left Harvey at his hotel James said to Anne, 'Why didn't you tell me? What am I going to say to the others?'

She just smiled. 'Don't say anything to them. Ask them to the wedding and say my mother's American, that's all. And James, you must think of a plan. He still has to give you

'James, come in and meet my father.'

$250,000 more. That hasn't changed, just because he's my father.'

When Stephen spoke to them all next time he said it was a little more than that in fact: $250,101.24.

CHAPTER FIVE

Everyone was waiting to hear James's plan.

'It's nearly ready,' he said. 'But first I have something to tell you and then I hope you'll agree to wait for a few weeks before we use my plan.'

'You're getting married,' said Jean-Pierre.

'That's right and I want you all to come to the wedding in Boston on August 3rd. Anne's mother is American, you see. Anne lives in London but her mother will be very happy if she gets married at home. Then we're going on holiday and we'll be back in England on August 25th. My plan starts on September 15th. Is that OK?'

Everyone agreed.

'There are some things that you can work on before then. Stephen, you must learn all about the price of gold in every country during the next month. Robin, I shall need seven telephones and a computer in my flat and you must know how to use the computer. Jean-Pierre you must learn about buying and selling dollars.'

He gave them some papers to study. Then he gave them their tickets to Boston: they were all flying there on the afternoon of August 2nd.

'We're staying in the same hotel on August 2nd. Your job is to make sure I arrive at the church on time on the 3rd.'

♦

Anne met them at Boston airport and they drove to the hotel together. When the others left James and Anne together, she asked him, 'Do they know about my father?'

He laughed. 'No, it's going to be a big surprise for them.'

'And is your plan ready, James?'

'Almost. It's going to start on September 15th.'

'I win then. Mine's for tomorrow,' said Anne, but she didn't tell James what her plan was.

♦

The next morning Stephen, Robin and Jean-Pierre stood outside the church waiting for Anne. When she got out of the car in her wedding dress they thought she looked very beautiful. When her father got out behind her and stood at her side their faces went red, then white. They couldn't move, they were so surprised. Harvey and Anne walked past them, into the church.

'Why didn't James tell us?' asked Stephen.

'He didn't recognize us,' said Robin.

'We all looked so different every time he saw us,' said Jean-Pierre.

'We must try not to stand too near to him at the party after the wedding,' said Stephen. 'If he talks to us maybe he will recognize our voices.'

'He'll want to talk to his friends, I hope, not us,' said Robin.

After the wedding everyone went to Harvey's house for the party. James's three friends drank champagne in a quiet corner and were very careful not to get too near to Harvey.

After the dinner James had to say a few words to everyone and Harvey did too. Then he gave Anne an envelope.

'This is a little wedding present, my dear, from your mother and me,' he said.

When she got out of the car in her wedding dress they thought she looked very beautiful.

Anne found Stephen and gave him the envelope.

When Anne looked inside, there was $250,000.

'Thank you, Daddy. I promise James and I will use it for something very special.'

When she showed it to James he was very surprised.

'You know what I'm going to do with it, don't you?' she asked him, and he smiled.

Anne found Stephen and gave him the envelope.

What a girl,' said Robin, while they looked at the money. 'Now, Professor, what do you think of that?'

Stephen laughed.

'I think we still have to get another $101.24 from him.'

♦

Anne and James were almost ready to leave for their holiday. Everyone wanted to see them get into their car and drive away. Suddenly Harvey said, 'Why do I have to think of everything?'

He turned round, saw Stephen and walked up to him.

'Rosalie is just going to leave and there are no flowers for her. They haven't arrived yet. Go to the flower shop along the road and buy some, will you? But hurry.'

Stephen hurried away from the people at the front of the house and Robin and Jean-Pierre ran after him.

At the back of the house, he stopped when he saw lots of beautiful flowers in Harvey's garden. He started taking them and told the others to help.

They returned to the front of the house just when Anne and James walked to their car. Stephen gave Harvey the flowers.

'Wonderful, my favourite flowers. How much did they cost?'

'100 dollars,' said Stephen quickly.

Harvey gave him the money and Stephen went back to Robin and Jean-Pierre.

Jean-Pierre laughed. 'Well, we got a bottle of very good champagne instead.'

James and Anne drove away and everyone started saying goodbye to Harvey and his wife. But Stephen, Robin and Jean-Pierre stayed away from him – they still didn't want him to recognize them. They quickly found a taxi to take them back to the hotel. When they drove away Robin saw that Jean-Pierre had a bottle of Harvey's champagne under his jacket and when they got into the hotel they enjoyed it together.

'It's a pity we didn't get that last $1.24,' said Stephen.

Jean-Pierre laughed. 'Well, we got a bottle of very good champagne instead.'

Four down: not a penny more and only a few pennies less than the $1,000,000 that they lost.

♦

They flew back to London the next day and Robin bought a newspaper at the airport. They took a taxi to Jean-Pierre's gallery and on the way Robin read his newspaper.

Suddenly he shouted, 'My God, it's not possible!'

They all looked at him in surprise and he started to read from the newspaper.

'"Prospecta Oil shares suddenly went up to £5.25 yesterday after another company found oil near the place where Prospecta were looking." Our shares now cost more than we paid for them and they're still going up. So we haven't lost our money after all . . . Harvey didn't steal it.'

'Oh no! What do we do now?' asked Jean-Pierre.

'Well,' said Stephen. 'I guess we'll have to think of a plan to give it all back to Harvey.'

EXERCISES

Vocabulary Work

Look back at the dictionary words in this story and make sure you understand each word.

shares	company	gallery
Lord	expert	races
casino	champagne	operate
fainted	telegram	private
Professor	gown	recognize

1 a Which word means 'someone who knows all about a subject'?
  b Which word means 'belonging to one person'?
  c Which word means 'to see someone and remember who they are'?
  d Which word is for something that you wear?
  e Which word means 'what you get if you buy part of a business'?
  f Which word is for an expensive drink from France?
  g Which word is for something that you send to someone?
  h Which word is for a place where you can play cards for money?

2 a Which of the dictionary words goes with each of these three-word groups?
  a knife hospital blood
  b business shares money
  c first run horses
  d hot fall white
  e pictures expensive sell

Comprehension

Chapter 1

1 How did David Kesler first know there was a problem with Prospecta Oil?
2 Who told Stephen about Harvey Metcalfe?
3 Who was the first one to think Stephen's idea was good?

Chapter 2

4 How did Jean-Pierre know when to put the Van Gogh into the window?
5 What did Harvey do that surprised them all?
6 Who was last person to get a glass of champagne in the Dorchester hotel?

Chapter 3

7 Why did Harvey feel ill at the casino?
8 What did James do in the Monte Carlo plan?
9 How did Harvey know what happened to him after he fainted?

Chapter 4

10 What was special about the day Stephen wanted Harvey to go to Oxford?
11 Why couldn't Harvey wear the gown he saw in the shop?
12 Why was James surprised when he met Anne's father?

Chapter 5

13 What did Stephen think they should try not to do at the wedding? Why?
14 Why did Stephen take the flowers from Harvey's garden?
15 Why did the price of Prospecta Oil shares go up again?

Discussion

1 Which plan do you think was the most exciting or dangerous, and why?

2 Do you think James really had a plan? How do you think he planned to get the other $250,000?

Writing

1 Think about the way that David Kesler felt when Stephen and the others lost their money. Write a short letter from David in New York to Stephen to explain what happened and say how sorry he is (about 100 words).

2 Write a few sentences about each of these people:

a Harvey Metcalfe b Anne Summerton c Stephen Bradley

Review

1 Who was your favourite person in the story and why?

2 Which part of the story surprised you most?